ALFIE TAKES ACTION

KAREN WALLACE
ILLUSTRATED BY ELLIE O'SHEA

To Sophie, another star,
with love, K.W.

BLOOMSBURY EDUCATION
Bloomsbury Publishing Plc
50 Bedford Square, London, WC1B 3DP, UK

BLOOMSBURY, BLOOMSBURY EDUCATION and the Diana logo are
trademarks of Bloomsbury Publishing Plc

First published in Great Britain in 2010 by A & C Black, an imprint of Bloomsbury Publishing Plc
This edition published in Great Britain in 2018 by Bloomsbury Publishing plc

A catalogue record for this book is available from the British Library

ISBN: PB: 978-1-4729-5059-8; ePDF: 978-1-4729-5639-2; ePub: 978-1-4729-5638-5

2 4 6 8 10 9 7 5 3 1

Printed and bound in China by Leo Paper Products, Heshan, Guangdong

All papers used by Bloomsbury Publishing Plc are natural, recyclable products from wood grown
in well managed forests. The manufacturing processes conform to the environmental regulations of
the country of origin.

To find out more about our authors and books visit www.bloomsbury.com
and sign up for our newsletters

Chapter One

Alfie was a meerkat who lived in
the desert with his mum and dad,
his brothers and sisters, his aunts
and uncles and most of his cousins.

Every morning, Alfie's mum woke up before dawn and told her family what to do. The jobs were always the same. First, babysitting, which meant looking after the little meerkats so they didn't run away.

Second, digging, which meant making
lots of tunnels to the nest.

And third, watching out for enemies, which meant standing on a big rock trying to spot eagles with sharp beaks or foxes with big teeth.

When she had given everyone a job,
Alfie's mum always said the same thing.
"GO, TEAM! GO!"

And Alfie's dad always said, "AND NO DAYDREAMING!"
He didn't actually *look* at Alfie. But Alfie knew his dad was talking to him. None of his brothers or sisters or cousins had ever had a daydream in their lives!

Chapter Two

One day, everything went wrong.
Alfie forgot about the little meerkats he
was looking after and they all ran away.

He started digging a tunnel to the
nest, but the roof fell down on top of
his uncle George.

Worst of all, a nasty bird almost ate his sister Fluff because Alfie was daydreaming.

"Alfie!" cried his mum. "We're supposed to be a *team*. What shall I do with you?" Alfie stared at his feet. "I could just stay by the nest and eat insects," he said. And Alfie's mum said it was the best idea he'd ever had.

The next morning, Alfie sat on a rock, trying to forget about his nasty sisters. Fluff had called him weird. Twitch said he was silly.

And Crumpet laughed and told him he wasn't a *proper* meerkat.

Alfie let out a big sigh.
"Cheer up," said a deep voice. "It can't
be that bad."

An old dog was standing by the rock.
"My name's Bongo," he said.
Bongo pointed to a big black scorpion.
"And this is my friend, Snapper."

Alfie didn't know what to say. The only thing he knew about scorpions was that they were good to eat!

Chapter Three

"W-w-what do you want?" spluttered Alfie.

"Nothing." Bongo pricked up his ears. "We thought you looked sad."

Snapper waggled his claws. "And we want to be friends."

"F-f-friends?" squeaked Alfie.
Meerkats didn't need friends. They had each other.
"What would I do with friends?"

"Friends have adventures together,"
said Snapper. "See that sand dune over
there? Something exciting is happening
on the other side!"

Alfie's eyes lit up. He *loved* exciting
things! "Can I have a look?" he asked.
Bongo laughed. "Come with us!"

Alfie followed Bongo and Snapper to the top of the sand dune.
What he saw on the other side made him fall back with a *thump*!

Chapter Four

A herd of monsters were sitting in a circle. They had flat backs and two eyes that stuck out in front. Something that looked like an enormous stick insect was sitting on top of one.

Alfie climbed on top of a thorn bush
to get a better look.

Creatures on two legs were running around the monsters. Some were peering into black boxes. Others were talking to furry things on the end of short poles.

Alfie nearly fell out of the thorn bush.
One of the creatures was pointing a
black box straight at him!

"Bongo!" Alfie squeaked. "What's going on down there?"

"There's only one way to find out!" cried the old dog, and he raced off across the sand with Snapper holding onto his ear.

Two minutes later, they were hiding behind a rock near the monsters. "W-w-what are those th-th-things?" gasped Alfie.

Chapter Five

Bongo whispered in Alfie's ear. "The monsters are trucks," he explained. "The stick insects are TV aerials, and the two-legged creatures are cameramen who make films."

Alfie blinked. "*What*?"

"Tell him, Snapper," said Bongo.

So Snapper told him about films and television and cameramen.

"Wow," said Alfie. "That's *incredible*!"

"Ssh," growled Bongo. "Here's company."

A big man and a small man sat down. "Are you *sure* the meerkat we saw just now is the one you've been watching all week?" asked the big man.

"Positive," said the small man. "He's different from the others. Sometimes I even think he's daydreaming!"

The big man chewed his lip. "And you really want to make a film about him?"

"Sure do," said the small man. "Remember *Super Snake*?"

"That film about the viper?" asked the big man. "Of course I do – it was brilliant!"

The small man grinned. "This one's going to be even better."

"OK," said the big man. "If you're so sure, we'll come back here tomorrow."
"Trust me," said the small man. "I know a star when I see one."
Alfie's eyes nearly popped out of his head!

Chapter Six

When the men had gone, Bongo turned to Alfie. "Did you hear that?" he cried. "He wants to make *you* a film star!"

"I don't get it," said Alfie. "Why me?"
"Because you're different," said
Snapper. "And you've got what it takes.
Now grab some sleep and we'll meet
back here at dawn. Those cameramen
are going to get the sight of their lives!"

Alfie's sisters were sitting by a rock.
"Had a nice day?" asked Fluff.
"All right for some, sitting around
eating insects," said Twitch.
"*We've* been doing jobs," said Crumpet.

"So what?" said Alfie, with a shrug.
"Tomorrow, *I'm* going to be a film star."

"You've been daydreaming again, dear," said Alfie's mum, from behind the rock.

"No, I haven't," said Alfie. "A man on the other side of that sand dune is going to make a film about me."

Alfie's mum went crazy. "Humans! Into the tunnel!" she barked.
And within seconds, all the meerkats had disappeared!

Chapter Seven

Alfie crept out of the nest while the other meerkats were asleep. It was still dark, but there was enough moonlight for him to find his way to the thorn bush.

"OK," said Bongo. "Now this is the plan... Go back and tell your family that humans are attacking the sand dune." "That'll get them going!" said Snapper with a chuckle.

Sure enough, as the sun began to rise, Alfie's mum led her family onto the sand dune. They jumped up and down, shook their paws and squeaked their heads off.

It was a meerkat war dance!

When the cameramen were almost at
the top of the sand dune, Bongo pushed
Alfie forward.

"Do it!" he cried. "This is your chance!"

Chapter Eight

Every bone in Alfie's body was shaking.
"Do *what*?" he wailed.
"Pretend you're a general and this is a
battle," hissed Snapper.
"But I'm a meerkat,"
said Alfie.
"I said *pretend*,"
Snapper shouted
back. "You're
a film star!
This is
television!"

Alfie had no idea what a general was,
so he did a few tricks instead. He
flipped over backwards...

walked on his hands...

and waved his legs in the air.
As the sun rose, his fur shone silver
and the sand in the air glittered like
diamonds. The cameramen were
amazed. Alfie was brilliant!

The first time the meerkats saw *Alfie, King of the Desert* everyone clapped and whistled. But Alfie's sisters cheered louder than anybody.

"You're wonderful," said Alfie's mum,
giving him a hug.

"He's the greatest," agreed Bongo.
"A mega film star," added Snapper.

Alfie grinned from ear to ear. For the
first time in his life, he felt *fantastic*.
And, best of all, this wasn't a daydream.
Every single bit of it was true!